Arctic Adventure

Written by Roderick Hunt

Illustrated by Alex Brychta

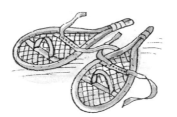

OXFORD
UNIVERSITY PRESS

Wilf was staying with Chip. It was very hot.

"It's too hot to sleep," said Chip.
"I wish we were in the Arctic,"
said Wilf. "It's cold there."

Suddenly, the magic key began
to glow. It took them into an
adventure.

The key took Chip and Wilf to
the Arctic. There was snow
everywhere.

The snow felt cold. "Brrrr!" said
Chip. "Now, I'm freezing."

Wilf saw a girl. "Help!" he called.
"We are freezing in this snow."

The girl came over. "You need some
warm clothes," she said.

"My name is Oona," said the girl.
"Put these clothes on."

"Now you can help me catch
some fish," said Oona.

"You can't catch fish in the snow,"
said Chip.

"I can," said Oona.

There was ice under the snow.
Under the ice was the sea. Oona
made a hole and they started to fish.

Soon, they had five fish.

Suddenly, Chip saw a polar bear. "Run!" he gasped. "It's going to eat us!"

Chip and Wilf ran.

"It's hard to run in the snow," panted Wilf.

"Stop!" called Oona. "The bear just wants some fish."

"She's only a cub, and she's lost,"
said Oona. "I've been helping my
dad to find her."

The cub ate the fish and soon
fell asleep.

"I'll call Dad now," said Oona.

Oona's dad came. "Well done, Oona," he said. "Now we can get the cub back to her mother."

They put the cub on a sled and
set off across the snow.

"The cub needs her mother,"
said Oona. "She hasn't learned
to hunt yet."

They saw a big bear on the ice.
"Is that her mother?" asked Wilf.

The mother bear gave a roar.
Then she dived into the sea and
swam to her cub.

"I'm glad we helped the cub find her mother," said Oona.

"I'm glad I'm not a polar bear!"
said Chip.

Just then, the key began to glow.

"That was a cold adventure,"
said Wilf.

"But it's still hot!" said Chip.

Think about the story

How did Oona catch the fish?

Why did the bear cub need her mother?

Why do you think people want to help polar bears?

If you were very hot, how would you cool down? If you were very cold, how would you keep warm?

A maze

Help the mother bear find her way to her cub.

**Useful common words repeated in this story and
other books in the series.**

across adventure back called catch clothes
everywhere find girl glad soon suddenly very were
Names in this story: Chip Oona Wilf